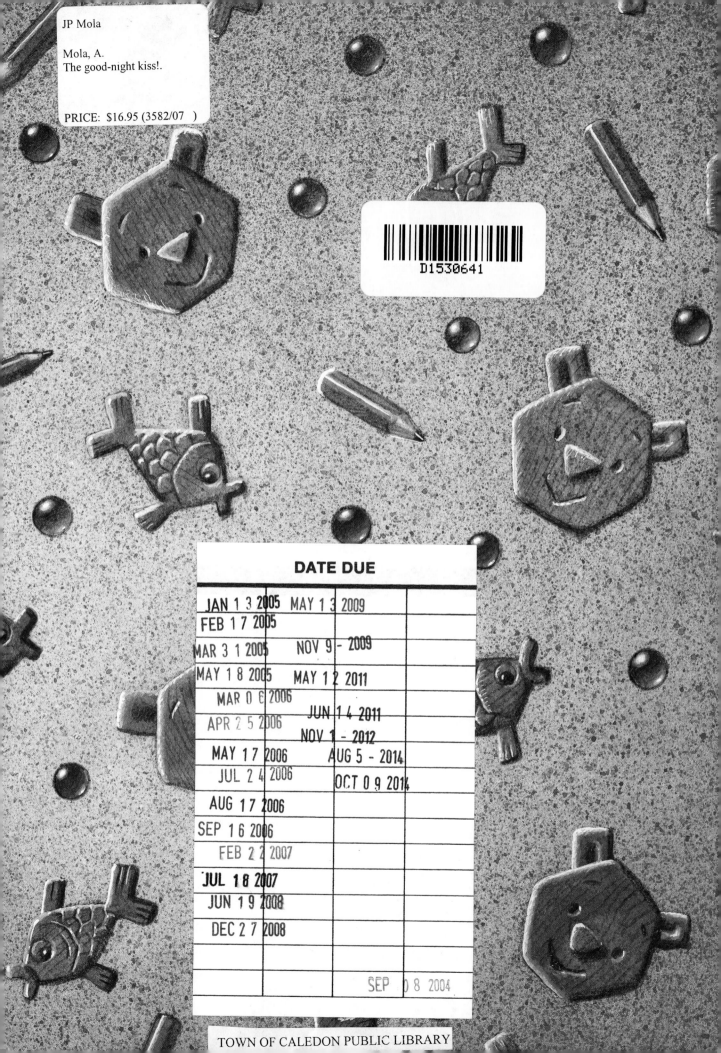

D1530641

THE GOOD-NIGHT KISS!

By Astrid Mola

Illustrated by Wahed Khakdan

Translated by J. Alison James

PARKLANE PUBLISHING

HAUPPAUGE, NEW YORK

One day Bear invited his friend Fox over to spend the night. When it was time for bed they went upstairs, but they did not stop playing. They were so noisy that Grandpa came up.

"Enough!" said Grandpa. "Stop your romping. It's time to go to sleep."

"But we're not tired," Bear said.

"We don't need to sleep," said Fox.

"Everyone needs sleep," said Grandpa. "Even you two."

"I'm wide awake," Bear said.

"Me too," said Fox. "I could run across the woods and back right now."

"Hmm," said Grandpa, "that could be a problem." He thought for a moment. "I have an idea. I'll give you a good-night kiss."

"Why?" asked Bear. "How could that help?"

"This is no ordinary good-night kiss," said Grandpa. "It's a *wandering* kiss. After I give it to you, you have to imagine who it might wander to next."

So Grandpa kissed Bear on the cheek and tucked them both in bed.

Bear tried to give the kiss to Fox.

"NO!" cried Fox. "Not me!" He jumped out of bed and ran around the room to escape the kiss.

Bear stopped chasing Fox and climbed back up in bed.

"Who should I give my kiss to, then?" he asked, feeling sad.

Fox's eyes grew bright. "If it were me," he said, "I'd give a kiss to Beaver. She's so sweet. I wouldn't mind giving her a kiss."

"You can't," said Bear, as he imagined them running through the woods after Beaver. "The kiss is mine to give."

"But will she take it?" Fox asked him.

"No," said Bear. "She won't stop running!"

"Then just give her a tiny little kiss on her back," said Fox. "She won't even feel it until it is too late."

"Good idea," said Bear.

"Who can Beaver give the kiss to?" Bear asked.
"Wolf!" cried Fox.
"No way," said Bear. "She's afraid of Wolf."

"No, she's not," said Fox. "She's really brave. She'll pucker up and kiss Wolf right above his drooling fangs—*smackers*—right on the nose!"

"Yeah," said Bear, "and the kiss will confuse Wolf so much, he'll give it away to . . ."

"Hedgehog!" cried Fox. "Spiny, prickly Hedgehog. Ouch!"

"And Wolf's kiss is so wet and slobbery, Hedgehog will run around all day trying to clean his spines."

"But then what?" Fox said. "Hedgehog has the kiss. Who will Hedgehog give it to?"

"I know," said Bear. "Mouse!"

"But Mouse is so small," said Fox. "Won't she be afraid?"

"Of course," said Bear. "She'll tremble with fear."

"Poor thing," said Fox.

"Yes," said Bear. "But who does Mouse kiss next?"

"Me!" said Fox.

"What?" said Bear. "You?"

"Yes, me," said Fox.

"Can't be," said Bear.

"Why not?" asked Fox.

"Well, okay," said Bear. "So?"

"So what?" asked Fox.

"So who are you going to kiss?" Bear asked.

"Oh, that," said Fox. "I know! I'll kiss Beaver."

"You can't!" said Bear.

"Why not?" asked Fox.

"She's already been kissed."

"Oh," said Fox. "You're right. Okay, you decide who I have to kiss then."

"Okay," said Bear. "You have to kiss . . . Skunk!"
"No way!" cried Fox.
"You said I could pick," said Bear.

"Okay," said Fox. "I'll hold my nose and kiss him fast—there. Done."

"Yuuuuuuck!" said Bear. "Did you smell him?"

"I kissed his *nose*, not his tail!" Fox said.

Fox and Bear rolled on the bed giggling.

"Who will Skunk kiss?" Bear asked when he stopped laughing.

"Mrs. Skunk," said Fox. "Everyone else would run away."

"Mrs. Skunk is friends with Badger," said Bear, "so she'll give the wandering kiss to him. Badger lives underground, so he'll take the kiss down a tunnel."

"Cool!" said Fox.

"And Badger kisses Mole," said Bear, "down inside his tunnel."

"And Mole can't see well so he kisses slimy Snail."
"Yuck," said Fox with a big yawn. "His mouth will
be slimy all day."

"Who does Snail kiss?" wondered Bear. "I guess he could go kiss Grasshopper. What do you think, Fox? Does Snail kiss Grasshopper? Fox? Hello?"

But Fox's eyes were closed. He was fast asleep.

Bear gave Fox a gentle kiss on the cheek. "There," he said. "You get to keep the wandering kiss."

Then Bear curled up next to his friend and fell right to sleep.